A Note to Parents

Reading books aloud and playing word games are two valuable ways parents can help their children learn to read. The easy-to-read stories in the **My First Hello Reader! With Flash Cards** series are designed to be enjoyed together. Six activity pages and 16 flash cards in each book help reinforce phonics, sight vocabulary, reading comprehension, and facility with language. Here are some ideas to develop your youngster's reading skills:

Reading with Your Child

- Read the story aloud to your child and look at the colorful illustrations together. Talk about the characters, setting, action, and descriptions. Help your child link the story to events in his or her own life.
- Read parts of the story and invite your child to fill in the missing parts. At first, pause to let your child "read" important last words in a line. Gradually, let your child supply more and more words or phrases. Then take turns reading every other line until your child can read the book independently.

Enjoying the Activity Pages

- Treat each activity as a game to be played for fun. Allow plenty of time to play.
- Read the introductory information aloud and make sure your child understands the directions.

Using the Flash Cards

- Read the words aloud with your child. Talk about the letters and sounds and meanings.
- Match the words on the flash cards with the words in the story.
- Help your child find words that begin with the same letter and sound, words that rhyme, and words with the same ending sound.
- Challenge your child to put flash cards together to make sentences from the story and create new sentences.

Above all else, make reading time together a fun time. Show your child that reading is a pleasant and meaningful activity. Be generous with your praise and know that, as your child's first and most important teacher, you are contributing immensely to his or her command of the printed word.

—Tina Thoburn, Ed.D.
Educational Consultant

Copyright © 1996 by Nancy Hall, Inc.
All rights reserved. Published by Scholastic Inc.
MY FIRST HELLO READER!, CARTWHEEL BOOKS, and the
CARTWHEEL BOOKS logo are registered trademarks of Scholastic Inc.
The MY FIRST HELLO READER! logo is a trademark of Scholastic Inc.

Library of Congress Cataloging-in-Publication Data

Hall, Kirsten.
    At the carnival / by Kirsten Hall; illustrated by Laura Rader.
        p.   cm.—(My first hello reader!)
    "Cartwheel books."
    "With flash cards."
    Summary: A boy's mother reminds him to stay close as they enjoy the rides at a carnival. Includes related vocabulary activities.
    ISBN 0-590-68994-0
    [1. Carnivals—Fiction. 2. Mothers and sons—Fiction. 3. Stories in rhyme.]
    I. Rader, Laura, ill. II. Title. III. Series.
PZ8.3.H146At   1996
[E]—dc20   96-1468
                                                              CIP
                                                              AC
12 11 10 9 8 7 6   8 9/9 0 1/0

Printed in the U.S.A.

First Scholastic printing, August 1996

AT THE CARNIVAL

by Kirsten Hall
Illustrated by Laura Rader

My First Hello Reader!
With Flash Cards

SCHOLASTIC INC.

New York   Toronto   London   Auckland   Sydney

A carnival!

Stay by my side.

Stay by my side

for every ride!

A rocket ship!

A bumper car!

Stay by my side, and don't go far!

A water slide!

A water slide!

My favorite ride!

A merry-go-round!

Around and around...

I'm lost!

I'm lost!

And now I'm found!

Around and around we ride
and ride.

Now, don't go far! Stay by
my side!

Rebus Words

Can you recognize these words from the story?

+ nival = ?

+ et = ?

r + + d = ?

Opposites

Opposites are words that mean something completely different.

For each word on the left point to its opposite on the right.

go   far

lost   up

near   found

down   stop

Carnival!

Point to five things that are wrong at this carnival.

Rhyme Time

Look at the words and pictures in each row. Point to the picture that rhymes with each word.

far

by

now

pocket

So Many Rides

Which is your favorite carnival ride?

Does it go fast or slow?

Does it go up and down?

Does it go around and around?

Why do you like it?

Answers

(Rebus Words)

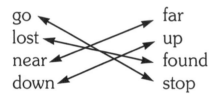 + nival = carnival

+ et = rocket

r + + d = ride

(Opposites)

go   far
lost   up
near   found
down   stop

(Carnival!)

These things are wrong:

(Rhyme Time)

far   (car)

by   (eye)

now   (cow)

pocket   (rocket)

(So Many Rides)

Answers will vary.